I know, it's a bad idea to hug a friend
I know, how this warm embrace is going to end

**A good fart these days is hard to hide
Shoots off at the worst time
A good fart these days is hard to hide
They drive me mental, these farts of mine**

**A good fart these days is hard to hide
Toots off at the worst time
A good fart these days is hard to hide
They're accidental, these farts**

Oh, these farts of mine

A good fart
A good fart

Achy Breaky Heart / Conspiracy Theorist Song

Original by Billy Ray Cyrus

You can wear your mask, obey and never ask
You can get a booster every day
Or you can wash your hands and keep at a distance
Whatever makes you happy, feeling safe
You don't get I'm wise, I've opened up my eyes
I've seen the truth behind all this fake news
Not much more than a cold, it just affects the old
I'm all about being free, you just do you

Don't doubt I'm smart, I'm really very smart
I know things I don't understand
My IQ's off the charts, I'm super highly smart
I've got the bestest logic in the land

You live life in fear, but me, my mind is clear
I don't care-if-you-have a PHD
I know much more than Fauci, cause I sit on my couch and
Absorb whatever's on my Facebook feed
You can try to scare me, saying I must take care -
I'll guzzle Ivermectin like cheap wine
You say the risk is true, but I won't believe you
Cause my cousin's neighbour's girlfriend was just fine

Don't doubt I'm smart, I'm really very smart
I don't care for academia
My IQ's off the charts, I'm super highly smart
Cause I have researched social media
Don't doubt I'm smart, I'm really very smart
Believe all I see on TV
My IQ's off the charts, I'm super highly smart
It all is just a big conspiracy

Contents

A Good Heart / A Good Fart	2
Achy Breaky Heart / Conspiracy Theorist Song	4
Africa / Stamina	5
All Through The Night / Snoring Song	7
Baby One More Time / Menopause Song	9
Bette Davis Eyes / Sweaty, Abrasive Thighs	11
Black Or White / Cat Song	13
Bohemian Rhapsody / Bohemian Catsody	15
Bohemian Rhapsody / Menopause Rhapsody	18
Dancing Queen / Expanding Jeans	21
Don't Stop Believin' / Can't Stop The Sneezin'	23
Drive / The Introvert's Song	24
Footloose / You Choose	25
Free Fallin' / Cold Callin'	27
Girls Just Wanna Have Fun / This Girl KNOWS How To Have Fun	29
Heart Of Glass / House Of Cats	31
Hello / Forgotten Password Song	33
Hopelessly Devoted To You / Hopelessly Devoted To Food	36
House Of The Rising Sun / The Housework's Never Done	37
I Got You Babe / I Got Toothache	38
I Will Always Love You / I Will Always Love Food	40
I Will Survive / I Won't Survive With No Wi-Fi	42
It's Raining Men / It's Ageing, Men	44
Killing Me Softly / Making His Coffee	47
Lady In Red / Lazy In Bed	49
Let's Get Physical / I'm So Critical	50
Livin' On A Prayer / Adulting Is Scary	52
Losing My Religion / Useless In The Kitchen	54
Mamma Mia / Song For Crafters	56
Piano Man / Trailers & Caravans	58
Respect / Retract	60
Rolling In The Deep / Folding Fitted Sheets	62
She's Got The Look / She Cannot Cook	65
Sound Of Silence / Sound Of Science	67
Stairway To Heaven / What A Cat Would Sing	69
Take My Breath Away / Take My Bread Away	71
Take On Me / Cat Version	72
The Logical Song / Dog Version	74
Time After Time / Time Flies Online	76
Time Of My Life / Prime Of My Life	78
Time Warp / Time Worn	80
Total Eclipse Of The Heart / Song For Older People	82
Vincent / Vintage	84
Vogue / Vague	85
Wake Me Up Before You Go-Go / Song For Introverts	87
Walking On Sunshine / Song About Ageing	90
Yesterday / Use-By Date	92
YMCA / Why Menstruate?	93
You Don't Own Me / Cat Version	95
You're The One That I Want / Money Song	97

A Good Heart / A Good Fart

Original by Feargal Sharkey

I make a lot of noises, though I do my best not to
Pressure builds up, then what are you gonna do?
High is the risk to let them out, the risk of getting heard
I hope they're too small to discern

Well I know 'cause I'm holding one in most the time
I know that they're tough to keep inside

A good fart these days is hard to hide
Toots off at the worst time
A good fart these days is hard to hide
They're accidental, these farts of mine

I'm in the supermarket and I feel a bubble brew
People all 'round - so what am I gonna do?
 I clench and grimace tightly, praying that no-one hears
Instead, a trumpet blares, please let me disappear

Well I know people say it's crude and not polite
I know with their amplitude - wish I was airtight!

Yes, a good fart these days is hard to hide
Blasts off at the worst time
A good fart these days is hard to hide
They're detrimental, these farts of mine

I live in trepidation of my backdoor breeze
Too scared to laugh, and terrified to sneeze
There's a new one always brewing - how can I tame my behind
'Cause a good fart these days is hard to hide

Africa / Stamina

Original by Toto

I used to go partying all night
Now I'm here in my slippers and my jammies - time to stay in
The TV blares - I get a fright
I never seem to get past half a movie before sedation!
The sun's gone down - there goes my day
Hoping to find some way to stay awake and keep some energy
Instead, I gently fade away
"Hurry, girl - it's off to bed for you!"

Just wanna stay up to cuddle and hang with you
There's nothing else to end my day that I would rather do
I miss the days when I had stamina
Gotta close my eyes, then I'm snoring - it's really bad (ooh ooh)

Of course, I'm up first morning light
Like star-crossed lovers, doomed with one awake, the other, fast asleep
How shall I remedy this plight?
Or else we'll be here tomorrow, I'll be comatose again while you watch TV
We're two ships passing in the night - frustrated at this sloth that I've become!

Just wanna stay up to cuddle and hang with you
There's nothing else to end my day that I would rather do
I miss the days when I had stamina
Gotta close my eyes, then I'm snoring - it's really bad (ooh ooh)

"Hurry, girl - it's off to bed for you!"

Just wanna stay up to cuddle and hang with you
There's nothing else to end my day that I would rather do
I miss the days when I had stamina
I miss the days when I had stamina
(I miss those days)

I've got the zest of a great-grandmama
Get home from work, put on my pyjamas
I'll stay awake.... It's just a nap, uh-huh.....
(Gotta close my eyes)
Gotta close my eyes, then I'm snoring - it's really bad (ooh ooh)

All Through The Night / Snoring Song

Original by Cyndi Lauper

All through the night
I lie awake, it's because of you
All through the night
I toss and I turn, don't know what to do

Oh, you're in your happy place
When the day breaks
How will I stay awake?

Explosive blast
Sonic attack
Your snoring thunders all through the night
And once you start
No turning back
Your engine's running all through the night
Until it ends
There is no end

All through the night
Elephant trumpets, chainsaw resounds
All through the night
Feels like I'm being chased by baying hounds
Oh, though I kick, you never stir
Sleep with a smile
And contentedly purr

Ferocious blast
Raucous attack
Your roaring thundering all through the night
I've come apart
My wits are cracked
My head is drumming all through the night
Until it ends
There is no end

Oh, and if your snores were not enough
You steal the blankets
I'm left in the buff
Ferocious blast
Constant attack
Outpouring, rumbling all through the night
And then you fart
My odds are stacked
What is this coming to through the night?

I'm round the bend
But if I send
You out, I'll be all alone tonight
You have my heart
I've got your back
I love you next to me through the night
Till I go deaf
There is no end

Oooooh
Oooooh
Oh, just be quiet
Just shut up
Let me go to sleep
Oooooh

Baby One More Time / Menopause Song

Original by Britney Spears

Oh, ladies, ladies
It's crazy, crazy

Oh, ladies, ladies, how was I supposed to know
I'm entering a nightmare
It's crazy, crazy, my body is letting go
I'm up to pee all night, yeah
Moody - don't get too close to me
Getting hairy, ovaries will shut down - menopause

My lower back is killing me
I'm full of stress - anxiety (don't touch me!)
Forget what to do, I lose my mind
I'm always cryin'
Just you wait till it's your time!

Oh, ladies, ladies
My body's a barbecue
That's randomly ignited
It's crazy, crazy
The sheets and shirts that I go through
It's not the way I planned it
Must pee - how'm I not yet empty?
I'm not 80, but I need to go again - this sux!

My lower back is killing me
I'm full of stress - anxiety (don't touch me!)
Forget what to do, I lose my mind
I'm always cryin'
Just you wait till it's your time!

Oh, ladies, ladies
My mind is hazy

Oh, ladies, ladies, how was I supposed to know?
It's crazy, crazy, my body is letting go

I must confess, I feel like a mess, it's wiping me out
What is happening to me?
I don't want hair here
Yes, I need some wine
Just you wait till it's your time!

My lower back is killing me
I'm full of stress - anxiety (don't touch me!)
Forget what to do, I lose my mind
I'm always cryin'
Just you wait till it's your time!

I must confess, I feel like a mess, it's wiping me out
What is happening to me?
I'm growing hair here
Yes, give me more wine
Just you wait till it's your time!

Bette Davis Eyes / Sweaty, Abrasive Thighs

Original by Kim Carnes

My hair is bleached and old
My lips, cracked and dry
I'm either hot or cold
I got wrinkles, but ain't wise

I ache more than I want to
Birthdays are not so nice
Where did the time all go?
I can barely recognise

And my knees, ooh, always freeze, ooh
And I clench each time I sneeze, ooh
The prognosis, well I know just how it
Ends but I will not miss
Out, I will not forego or play nice,
I'm here
And I'm full of life!

I got to get back home
To be in bed by 9
Without my glasses on
I got blurry, useless eyes

And please don't mumble when you
Talk, look me in the eyes
Otherwise I won't hear you
And you'll have to say it twice

Time will show you that all those who
Seem so fleet and young grow old too
It's atrocious how all roses wilt, it
Makes the beauty pros blush
I once valued youthful size -
I got
Sweaty, abrasive thighs

And my knees, ooh, always freeze, ooh
And I clench each time I sneeze, ooh
The prognosis, well I know just how it
Ends but I will not miss
Out, I will not forego or play nice,
I'm here
And I'm full of life!

And my knees, ooh
Always freeze, ooh
Careful sneeze, ooh
I got blurry, useless eyes

Time will show you
Wilted rose, ooh
You'll grow old too
You'll get sweaty, abrasive thighs

Black Or White / Cat Song

Original by Michael Jackson

Got a dilemma, need a new friend for me
I've heard their colours show personality
Some say that I'll be miserable
That a grey cat's always picking a fight

If you're thinkin' about being my kitty
Doesn't matter if you're black or white

They call the orange cats the friendliest ones
White cats are snobby, as for black ones - just run!
Now, I believe in equality and I think
That every colour's just right!

If you're thinkin' about being my kitty
Doesn't matter if you're black or white

Why is colour so special?
Why focus on this stuff?
I just want a sweet kitty
And each one is worthy of love
I won't judge by your colour
But personality
If you're up for adoption
You could be the right one for me

Protection
Stop fur discrimination
Causing grief in feline relations
It's a poor call on a tonal scale
Enough to make a cat swish its tail

See, it's not about pigments
They're figments, malignant
Every kitty needs
Our loving treatment
It's just a surface cover
I'm not going to define you by your fur colour

Won't label you as mean or sweet
From seeing if you're dark or you're light

'Cause if you're thinkin' about being my kitty
Doesn't matter if you're black or white
I said if you're thinkin' about being my kitty
Doesn't matter if you're black or white
If you're thinkin' about being my best friend
Doesn't matter if you're black or white

If black, if white
I won't judge you, kitty, no
If dark, if light

If black, if white
I won't judge you, kitty, no
If dark, if light

Bohemian Rhapsody / Bohemian Catsody

Original by Queen

Staying up all night
Race round the house at 3
Show you my backside
After nudging you to pet me
Obsessed with flies
A box half my size fits me

I choose to employ - you, now attend to me
Open the door, I'll come, then I'll go
Feed me now, don't be slow
Stalk you in the bathroom, privacy don't matter to me
To me

Mama,
Just killed a mouse
Ate it all except the head
That's your present on your bed
Mama, a sign of my love -
Why did you scream and throw it all away?

Mama, ooh
Didn't mean to make you cry,
I'll try to find a bird for you tomorrow,
So sit down, I'll sit on -
You - knead your legs to tatters

Too late - pat time is done
I've had enough, now I'm going to swipe you if you try
Don't you touch my body till I say so
Now, just leave me till I find a use for you

Water, ooh
"It's not fresh!" I'll cry
How could my dish be left five minutes or more?

I see a little silhouette under the quilt
I'll attack, won't hold back, thanks for sharing your big toe!
Teeth and claws and fighting, kick, kick, kick and biting glee

You're my prey-o!
Come and play-o!
I will scratch you,
Try to catch you
Now feed me and don't be slow
Or I will meowwwwww

I'll sharpen my claws on your new settee
Sleep on your keyboard - I claim your property
Remember your role is to wait on me
In I come, out I go, hurry up, don't be slow

Let me out! No, now I don't want to go
(Let me go!) I want out! Or do I want to go?
(Let me go!) Let me out! Or, maybe… I don't know
(I don't know!) In or out, who knows?
(I don't know!)(Never) Never gonna know
(Let me go) (Never) Maybe no (I don't know) Ah
YES, no, YES, no, YES, no, YES, YES, no

The door is closed, the door is open, what do I want, I don't know!
Just hurry up, you must do what I decide quickly
For me, serve me!

3am is my best time for racing around!
Now I'll sit on the table - crash things to the ground!
Oh, maybe, I'll let you stroke me, lady
Enough - now get out, I need some more solitude here

I'm the one who matters,
Anyone can see
The song of all cats is
Everyone exists to serve me….
Watch out for your big toe!

Bohemian Rhapsody / Menopause Rhapsody

Original by Queen

Is this my new life?
Irritability?
Shutting down inside
I can't sleep and am so itchy
Got sweaty thighs
This is my demise, you see….

I'm just a woman asking for sympathy
Because a hot flush comes, memory goes
Mood is high, then it's low
Every day, more hair grows where I don't want any to be
Poor me!

Mama
It's menopause
No more children can be bred
Now my ovaries are dead
Mama
No, it's not much fun
I once was hot in quite a different way!

Drama, oooh,
Don't know if I'll laugh or cry
I can't remember my plans for tomorrow,
And my 'drive' has all gone
My brain is feeling scattered…..

Too late, my prime has gone,
Bones shrinking in my spine,
Body's aching all the time
Good night - no, I won't sleep. Just got to go
Gonna toss and turn and pee the whole night through!

Sauna, ooh, (Oooh - where'd my fan go?)
I'm all cracked and dry
I can't stand heat and summer time at all!

I am a grumpy hot potato, yes I am
A hot flush, you just shush
Go and open a window!
Thunderbolts and lightning - don't cross me, I'm frightening, see

Just obey-oh,
All I say-oh
Do my way-oh
Or you'll pay-oh
Don't delay-oh - don't you know
I'm gonna blow-oh-oh-oh

I'm just a poor girl with a hot body
She's just a poor girl, nauseous and clammy
Just give her chocolate and wine, let her be
Magnesium for the bones, more pills for my hormones
This hot flush,
No - we will not let you go
This headache
This mood swing,
We will not let you go
No, no, no, no, no, no, no

Oh menopausa, menopausa, menopause, just let me go
This hellish club turns all women into wild banshees,
Banshees, banshees!

So you think you can stop age and turn back time
So you think that your fountain of youth won't run dry?
Oh, ladies, take it from me, poor ladies
It's going to get you, your time will soon come - be prepared!
OOOh-oooh-ooh oh yeah, oh yeah

My nerves are all shattered, always need to pee
Hairier and fatter,
Menopause is battering me
At least no more 'Aunt Flo'….

Dancing Queen / Expanding Jeans

Original by ABBA

Oooh
At first glance - Perfect size
I put them on for the night
Oooh, eat that grill
Lick plates clean
I need expanding jeans

Friday night, going to a show
Gotta eat first - where should we go?
A good meal's therapeutic
Deep fried chicken wings
Pizza with everything

After I've had some more Pad Thai
Feel a tightening in my fly
As my digestive juices
Start to do their thing
Waist-band is tightening

To ease my suffering
I need expanding jeans
When I eat
I might bust a seam!
Expanding jeans
I'm defeated by KFC - oh yeah!

At first glance
Perfect size
I thought they'd last for the night
Oooh, I've been filled -
Feel that squeeze
I need expanding jeans

They were tight when I put them on
Gone, my shape at age 21
Now, I look like my mother
I've got to undo
Gotta loosen my pants

How I wish that I had -
Looser, expanding jeans
When I eat
I'm a frightful scene
Expanding jeans
So I can eat some more ice cream - oh yeah!

Wore these pants
For the night
What to do now - they're too tight!
Oooh, got no will - power, see?

I need expanding jeans
I need expanding jeans

Don't Stop Believin' / Can't Stop The Sneezin'

Original by Journey

Just a rundown girl
Dosing up on Benadryl
She hates the flowers and the trees, being out in fresh air

Just a clogged up boy
Springtime robs him of his joy
Takes antihistamine with him everywhere

In winter I would get the flu
But know that spring was coming soon
All those flowers would pollenate
And I'd ahh and aaah and aaah and aaaaaaaachooo!

Dangers lurking
Up and down in every yard
Block my nose, stinging in my eyes

Dust mites, give me pills
My head's in a near explosion
Hide me somewhere that's airtight!

Can't stop the sneezin'
Got that bunged up feelin'
Spring time's evil

Can't stop the sneezin'
I'm gone
Spring hates people

Can't stop the sneezin'
I hate how I'm feelin'
Bring Benadryl

Drive / The Introvert's Song

Original by The Cars

Who wants to go out when it gets late?
Who thinks that Friday drinks are that great?

Pyjamas on, watching whatever's on, and now
I'm gonna just stay home tonight

Don't want to socialise, not at all
Just gives me butterflies - please don't call
Don't want to pay attention when you speak
I'd rather stay right here just with me

Pyjamas on, loving being alone, so now
I'm gonna just stay home tonight

True that I said I'd come - I regret
I'd rather be at home with my pets

Pyjamas on, my idea of fun, and now
I'm gonna just stay home tonight
Oh - got my pyjamas on, free from everyone
I'm gonna just stay home tonight

Footloose / You Choose

Original by Kenny Loggins

Been working so hard
These last years have scarred
You're sour - for what?
You unleash all you got

Don't care about feelings
So nasty, bringing us down
All words have meaning
Do you enjoy that big frown?

Your attitude is on you - you choose
Put yourself in our shoes
Please, just breathe
Why cut us to our knees?
Talk smack, attack
Trying to make us crack
Lose abuse
Kindness takes real guts to choose!

Demand what we do
You think it's all about you
Dig way down in your heart
You're burning, yearning for some

Somebody to like you
They won't when you're the bad guy
I'm trying to tell you
Being nice is something new to try

Tell me, why are you being so obtuse? You choose
Attitude's up to you
Oh, we all see

**Your actions are ugly
Sit tight - don't fight
You are not always right
Dude! You're rude!
Others are important too!**

(Oh-oh-oh-oh) Attitude
(Oh-oh-oh-oh) Up to you
(Oh-oh-oh-oh) You must choose

Why don't you turn things around?
Yes, turn that frown upside down
Don't give such anger control
Aaaah!

**It's all up to you! You choose
Get a fresh attitude
Please, just ease
Meanness kills like disease
Talk smack, attack
It just drives you off track**

**Lose abuse
Workers are all people too!
You choose
Attitude's up to you
We all see
Your actions are ugly
Sit tight - don't fight
You are not always right
Dude! You're rude!**

Why live in disgust? Get out of your rut
Stop being so unjust, leave it in the dust
Attitude adjust, give the mean a cut

Kindness takes real guts to choose!

Free Fallin' / Cold Callin'

Original by Tom Petty

Get a phone call during dinner
Who is this? Private number too
Do I know you? What's this 'bout insurance?
I'm eating now - no, thank you!

It's been a long day
Then my phone starts ringing
Without delay
You start pitching things hard
Now I'm just annoyed
'Cause I don't know you, caller
This is no joy
I don't want to take part

Don't agree
To cold calling
Annoys me
Cold calling

I'm kinda busy
Can I get your home details
And call you back
In a few hours' time?
Oh, you're not working
Then, why should that matter?
It's just your leisure
Like how you're now ruining mine!

**Don't call me
Cold calling
Let me be
Cold calling**

**Don't bug me
Cold calling
Give me peace
It's appalling
Don't call me**

Girls Just Wanna Have Fun / This Girl KNOWS How To Have Fun

Original by Cyndi Lauper

I'd come home in the morning light
But now it's my best thing to have an early bedtime
Chocolate and beer, I'll watch The Bachelor reruns
This girl knows how to have fun
This girl knows how to have fun

Won't see me out past nine o'clock at night
You'll find me in my garden in the morning light
Make sure I have a nice, hot cuppa at one
This girl knows how to have fun
Oh this girl knows how to have

Cause I know what I want
Some fun
Got another jigsaw done
This girl knows how to have fun
This girl knows how to have fun

Small joys are enough for this girl
Like reading and embroidery - come, give it a whirl
Don't wanna go out, rather nap in the sun
This girl knows how to have fun
Oh, this girl knows how to have

Cause I know what I want
Some fun
Got another Wordle done
This girl knows how to have fun
This girl knows how to have fun

This girl knows how to
How to have fun
Don't wanna
Please everyone

She knows how to, knows how to
This girl - this girl knows how to have fun
She'll keep her comfy things on
All expectations are gone
She'll sleep as soon as she's done

Heart Of Glass / House Of Cats

Original by Blondie

Once I really loved to go have a gas
Why go out? Stay home with my cats
Stroking and purring, scratch their behinds
Much prefer cats to humankind

Once I had nice stuff, now I've got felines
Scratched up couch, torn Venetian blinds
Now I'm always sneezing, got puffy eyes
Still prefer cats to humankind

Yes, it means
I've no risk of freezing; sat on all the time
Always do their bidding, I've been catnotized
Might seem crazy what I do, but it's so good
When they rub against you

Never get enough of their spunk and sass
Why go out? Stay home with my cats
Licking and chasing, show their behinds
Much prefer cats to humankind

Stay inside
Adorable companions keep me satisfied
If I hear you knocking, I might dart off and hide
This life is of my choosing, yeah

La, da, da, la, la, la, la, la, la, la, la
La, da, da, la, la, la, la, la, la, la, la
La, da, da, la, la, la, la, la, la, la
And now all my clothing is cat fur lined

Ooh, oh, ooh, oh Ooh, oh, ooh, oh x2

Once I really loved to go have a gas
Why go out? Stay home with my cats
Sleeping and darting, wiggling behinds
Much prefer cats to humankind
Ooh, oh, ooh, oh Ooh, oh, ooh, oh x2

Hello / Forgotten Password Song

Original by Adele

Oh, no - It's me!
You won't recognise my password
When I hit the ENTER key
I did not change anything
What is wrong with this computer?
It won't let me in

Oh, no - Recognise me!
Now you ask these stupid questions
To check my identity
What was that movie I liked?
I first filled this out an age ago
When I was 25

I chose something different
Uniqueness
It's now my demise

I can't get the password right
I've typed it out a thousand times
What to do? I'm sorry
I started with only one
But each site wants new things
My memory's coming undone

8 letters long - yes, I have tried
But still it won't be verified
I put numbers, symbols
And my Mom's maiden name
But when I press ENTER
The rejection stays the same
A locked door

Oh, no - Let me through
I've run out of combinations
I can't think of more, I'm sorry
Childhood pet?
Did that as well
Will I ever make it through this barrier?
Will it ever happen?

It's so secret
Don't know what it is
And I've tried too many times

I just want to override
It's really me! Let me inside!
Yes, it's mandatory
But now my patience is gone
I'm in purgatory
I can't find the right one

Which one was it? I can't decide
A hundred combos - yes, I've tried
You keep saying, 'No Entry'
I'm falling apart
It's your fault for wanting
A complex code at the start
I'm done for!

Ooh - can't take more
Ooh!

I can't get my password right
I'm giving up; I've tried and tried
Now I'm getting worried
I've got so much online
I'm in such a flurry
This is eating my time

Please, just let me get inside
I'm sure I've got my password right
Why is there a green light
Here by my CAPS LOCK key?
Let me press that button
Try again and let's see, oh…

Oh, I'm in!
Yay!
CAPS LOCK

Hopelessly Devoted To You / Hopelessly Devoted To Food

Original by Olivia Newton-John

Guess my pants aren't the first popped open
'Cause when I see a buffet, I
Must be the first to go
There's just no getting over food
I know my plate is overfilling
And I'll be up soon for Round two
Not hungry, but I'll eat - there's just so many things to chew
I'm hopelessly devoted to food

But now I'm getting too wide
I must cast old clothes aside
But, oh, smell that bread!
Hopelessly devoted to food
Everything just tastes much too good
Hopelessly devoted to food

My head is sayin', "Fool, you've eaten"
My eyes are sayin', "Don't say no"
Eat until it ends, self-control is overdue
I'm hopelessly devoted to food

But now my stomach aches, I
Must still try that apple pie
I'm so overfed
Hopelessly devoted to food

Everything just tastes much too good
Hopelessly devoted to food

House Of The Rising Sun / The Housework's Never Done

Original by The Animals

There is a house that's always clean
It sure as hell ain't this one
Yes, I should be doing
More, but it sparks no joy
No, my housework's never done

My mother was a stickler
She lived to keep clean
She'd dust and mop, then scrub non stop
I didn't inherit those genes

Now, the only thing I want to do
When I get home each day
Is to have 'me time' with a glass of wine
Not put your socks away

Another load of laundry
I just folded the last one
Vacuumed last week, what is this trickery?
My neat sanctuary now gone

The kind of house in magazines
Well, it sure as hell ain't this one
Yes, I should be doing
More, but it sparks no joy
No, my housework's never done

I Got You Babe / I Got Toothache

Original by Sonny & Cher

Since I was young, I can't say no
Go all out and eat this gateau
Sweet, gooey dough and toffee too
My mouth's all sticky, sugar flowing through

Ache
I got toothache
I got toothache

Volume control, Hundred percent
Shoot 'em up game, I don't know where time went
All through the night, I give all I've got
Stare at the screen, my eyes are all bloodshot

Ache
I got headache
I got headache

Rights are ours - do your thing
Misconstrue results they bring
That's why I'm sad when it's found
I wasn't prepared, and now run aground

I want my way, been nice too long
I don't care, I'm right, you're always wrong
Yes, I'll belittle you all the time
I'll get my fill of me, myself and I

Ache
I got heartache
I got heartache

No-one wants to hold my hand
No-one seems to understand
Nobody takes care of me
No-one has much sympathy

I feel ill but not contrite
'Cause I do just what I like
Consequence of letting go
No-one warned me of this though

I got toothache
I got toothache
I got headache
Ooh, bellyache
I got backache
I got earache
I got heartache
I'm a headache

I Will Always Love You / I Will Always Love Food

Original by Dolly Parton

I like good steak
Guacamole and chips entree
Potatoes, risotto
Take me to an - all you can eat buffet

And I will always love food
I will always love food

Food - it is so good - mmmm
Savoury sweet memories
No such thing as left-overs for me
Apple pie caught my eye
Yes, I know it's a want
Not a need

But I will always love food
I will always love food, oooh

I can't cope without French fries
And I hope for a cake to
Lick cream off
Feed me a doughboy - mmm
Warm stickiness
Yes, it gives me gas - but it's never enough

Cause I will always love food
I will always love food,
I will always love food,
I will always love food,
I will always love food,
I, I will always love food

Food
Oh, it tastes so good
Ooh - I'll always
I'll always love food

I Will Survive / I Won't Survive With No Wi-Fi

Original by Gloria Gaynor

At first I was afraid, I was petrified
I wondered how I'd ever live without it by my side
But you said it's just one night - surely I'd make it that long
Well you were wrong
I need my signal to be strong

We must go back
And leave this place
There's not a tower 'round for miles, it's like we're stuck in outer space
Why did I say yes to this walk, or think that camping was for me?
If I'd known for just one second I could not update my feed

Come on, let's go, or this is war
Must turn around now
'Cause I can't take it any more
Weren't you the one who promised Instaworthy sights?
But I can't post a reel
I might as well lay down and die

Oh, woe is I - I need Wi-Fi
Oh, I long to get more followers, take selfies, count the likes
Through my screen is how I live
I've got influence to give, but no Wi-Fi
I won't survive with no Wi-Fi

It's taking all the strength I have not to fall apart
But it has been at least three hours since I tapped a heart
And I spent so much freaking time and product, readying myself
What's the point, why?
I'm in a black hole - can't go live

Fans can't see me
What will they do?
They will forget that I exist and move on to somebody new
And so you think without my phone, you just expect me to be free
Well now, its influence is more than you could ever have on me

Come on, let's go, or I'm done for
Must turn around now
'Cause I can't take it any more
Weren't you the one who said this trail was really nice?
You knew I'd crumble!
What? Are you trying to make me die?

Oh, woe is I. I need Wi-Fi
Oh, I long to get more followers, take selfies, count the likes
Through my screen is how I live
I've got influence to give, but no Wi-Fi
I won't survive

Come on, let's go, I so abhor
I've run aground now
'Cause I can't take it any more
Weren't you the one who planned this 'romantic' surprise?
Well, get on Bumble!
That's right - you can't - there's no Wi-Fi!

Oh, woe is I. I need Wi-Fi
Oh, I long to get more followers, take selfies, count the likes
Through my screen is how I live
I've got influence to give, but no Wi-Fi
I won't survive with no Wi-Fi

It's Raining Men / It's Ageing, Men

Original by The Weather Girls

Your belt-line's slowly rising
Your belly is getting low
Your man-boobs are enormous
Where did that six-pack go?

It's a fright, oh, the worst time
When you can't get it up again
An eternity to make a pee
You're not the stud you were back then

It's called ageing, men!
Happens to ya!
It's that age when
Hair gets thin
You used to go out, have fun
Always look your best
Now a lemon has more zest

It's ageing, men
Caught up to ya!
It's changing men
Every specimen
Used to look so mean
Flab now where muscles have been

Bloody Mother Nature
Look at what she's done to you!
Now no younger women
Bat their eyes like they used to

Don't have a midlife crisis
It's one thing you can't defy
If your person is true, they'll stick with you
You're still their perfect guy!

It's ageing, men
We still love ya!
So don't complain
We are all has-beens
Men - happens to ya!
It's ageing, men, Ancient!

Eyesight fading
False teeth going in
When did this begin?
Can't hear much now
Don't you lose your head!
Better to dance than stay in bed

Get your act together
Others are all ageing, too
Soon it's time for heaven
But there's still lots that we can do
Don't think that you'll beat it
By buying a sports car
You don't have to impress anyone
We love you as you are!

You're ageing, men - Yeah

Your blood pressure is rising
Libido is getting low
You're no more an Adonis
Hair sprouts from your ears and nose!

It's alright, men, you'll be fine
Just take a blue pill or ten
For the first time in your history
You've gotta deal with ageing, men

It's called ageing, men!
Happens to ya!
It's that age when
Hair gets thin
You're ageing, men!
We're there with ya!
We're ageing, men, Oh, yeah!

It's ageing, men
We still love ya!
So don't complain
We're has-beens!
Just ageing, men!
Happens to ya!
It's ageing, men, Ancient!

It's ageing, men!
Happens to ya!
It's that age when
Hair gets thin
You're ageing, men!
We're there with ya!
We're ageing, men, Oh, yeah!

It's ageing, men
We still love ya!
So don't complain
We're has-beens!
Just ageing, men!
Happens to ya!
It's ageing, men, Ancient!

Killing Me Softly / Making His Coffee

Original by Roberta Flack

Grinding the beans takes him ages
Steaming the milk - my ears hurt
Making his coffee takes so long
Premium coffee - must be strong
Shaking the whole house and my nerves
Making his coffee takes so long

He goes into the kitchen
To make coffee in style
And so I grit my teeth
To suffer for a while
There goes my sleeping-in joy
Doesn't help to close my eyes

Grinding the beans takes him ages
Steaming the milk - my ears hurt
Making his coffee takes so long
Premium coffee - must be strong
Shaking the whole house and my nerves
Making his coffee takes so long

The house is filled with flavour
The beans, perfectly ground
His coffee makes him better
But must it be so loud?
I pray that he would finish
But that machine chugs on

Grinding the beans takes him ages
Steaming the milk - my ears hurt
Making his coffee takes so long
Premium coffee - must be strong
Shaking the whole house and my nerves
Making his coffee takes so long

Some might think I am lucky
Barista of my own
To give me fresh made coffee
In bed, right in my home
It's true that it sounds peachy
But I can't stand the stuff…

Grinding and chugging - outrageous
Shut off that steam - my ears hurt
Making his coffee takes so long
Like a jet engine - sounds so strong
Noisy so early, and what's worse
I don't like coffee. It's so wrong

Lady In Red / Lazy In Bed

Original by Chris De Burgh

I've never had enough of being snuggly in my bed each night
I'm never sick of eyes shut tight
I'm never rested well enough - at work, I'm in a stuporous trance
Waiting for the week to advance,
Saturday's my chance
And until then, I must keep persevering
Live on caffeine, give blank stares through bloodshot eyes
In the weekend, I'll

Be lazy in bed, quite ready to sleep - it's been a week!
It's noon - I don't care, just don't bother me
It's where I want to be
My blinds tightly closed to block out the sunlight
I just want to rest - I might get up tonight

I never feel like getting out of bed and going outside
It's never that much fun and I much prefer snoozing
I'd rather be away from people - under my covers, I'll hide
And with a great book at my side - that's how I'll spend my day!
And I will never ignore the feeling
Such a feeling of complete and utter sloth.
Every weekend I

Am lazy in bed, quite ready to sleep - it's been a week!
It's noon - I don't care, just don't bother me
It's where I want to be
My blinds tightly closed to block out the sunlight
I just want to rest - pretend that it's midnight

Being lazy is the best - leave me alone - good night
I'm lazy in bed x4
(*Hugs pillow*) I love you

Let's Get Physical / I'm So Critical

Original by Olivia Newton-John

I live, laugh and love, but I just don't like
Threaten with litigation
I know my rights - I'm always right
And I will cause a scene

The food's not to my taste at the restaurant
Got a hard seat at the movies
There's nothing left but to scream and shout
Now, get the manager for me!

I'm so critical, critical
I might just get physical
'Cause I'm egotistical
Throw a tantrum, rant and squawk,
I'll rant and squawk
Swoop down like an evil hawk

Always critical, critical
I'm apocalyptical
My outrage is biblical
I know best, so let me talk,
I'll rant and squawk
Your head's on the chopping block

I'm not patient, you're no good
Meet my needs because I'm entitled
I'm all worked up, no holding back
I'll speed dial the police!

I'm never coming back, I'll leave a bad review
For all the whole wide world to see
It doesn't take much to bring out
The animal in me

I'm so critical, critical
I'm gonna get physical
'Cause I'm egotistical
Throw a tantrum, rant and squawk,
I'll rant and squawk
Swoop down like an evil hawk

Always critical, critical
I'm apocalyptical
My outrage is biblical
I know best, so let me talk,
I'll rant and squawk
Your head's on the chopping block

I'm so critical, critical
Over things so minuscule
Don't look at me quizzically
Throw a tantrum, rant and squawk,
I'll rant and squawk
Managers will shake in shock
Like an animal, animal

I'm acting irrational
Totally implacable
Screeching like a mad macaque,
I'll rant and squawk
Nightmare for all those who work
Throw a tantrum, rant and squawk
Why am I the laughing stock?

Livin' On A Prayer / Adulting Is Scary

Original by Bon Jovi

Frantic in the car parking lot
Can't remember where
I parked, car is lost, it's tough, so tough
Out and in the public all day
Zip down on my pants
Why did no-one say? It sux, hmmm - so rough

You see, all this adulting comes with great cost
Spend half my time convinced I have to fake things a lot
Prove to all others that I am not - a hoax
What if I get caught?!

Oh, it's just not fair
Oh - givin' me a scare
Out of hand, just might make me swear
Oh - adulting is scary

Time to get my credit card bill
It's more than just scary - it makes me quite ill
So tough, it's tough
Traffic jam and I gotta pee
A restroom's up ahead, but when last has it been cleaned?
Hygiene!

Gotta make phone calls - I'm all in knots
Small talk and socialising all still scare me a lot
Don't mention spiders - I'm just distraught - enough
Oh, perish the thought!

**Oh, it's just not fair
Oh - givin' me a scare
Out of hand, might make me swear
Oh - adulting is scary - Adulting is scary**

We've got to hold on, ready or not
Grown up life throws us all the curve balls it's got

**Oh, it's just not fair
Oh - givin' me a scare
Out of hand, might make me swear
Oh - adulting is scary - Adulting is scary**

**Oh, it's just not fair
Oh - givin' me a scare
Out of hand, might make me swear
Oh - adulting is scary - Adulting is scary**

Losing My Religion / Useless In The Kitchen
Original by REM

My knife is bigger
My oven is too
I spend lots of money
The lengths that I will go to
To cook things really nice
Oh no, it's set too much
I messed it up

That's me, the food burner
That's me, my food's not liked
I'm useless in the kitchen
Trying to whip up a stew
And I don't know if I can do it
Oh no, I've added too much
I messed it up

I thought I'd be good at cooking
I thought that this was my thing
Now every meal just makes you cry

Got lots of blisters, my face is full of flour
I'm hiding my discretions
Lying about that thing you chewed
I'm a hurt, hot and blinded fool, fool
Oh no, it boiled too much
I messed it up

Consider this
Consider that we should go out to eat
It's hit or miss - and this
Might give you some disease,
What if my friends and family come?
We'll go to town
Oh - I've cooked enough

I thought that I heard you barfing
Okay, so don't eat that thing
You're really brave for even trying

Perhaps it was the cream
Or that cheese that went green

Might need the coroner
I give up - I'll not fight
I'm useless in the kitchen
Trying to feed all of you
And I don't think that I should do it
Oh no, it's come out tough
I've messed it up

I thought there's no knack to cooking
I thought we would eat like kings
I really don't want you to die!
But that was just a dream
Try - my - pie - die
That was just a dream

Just a dream
Just a dream, dream

Mamma Mia / Song For Crafters

Original by ABBA

I've been hoarding supplies since I don't know when
A sale's been advertised, time for shopping again

Look at my house, there is no more room
And my poor spouse sits surrounded by fabric rolls
Things have spiralled out of control

Just one sale and I forget everything
I must go and buy all the pretty things - woooh

Crafter here - here I go again
Tie dye - how can I resist you?
More ideas - gotta sew again
Buy, buy! Or one day I'll miss you

I am a needy artist
Projects are all half started
Why, my crafting mess just seems to grow
Now it's clear, now I really know
Time I try to let this clutter go...

Marie Kondo says keep only things that spark joy
But this lonesome earring is just too cute to destroy

Buttons and beads, wrapping paper stored
And I might need that old greeting card from Peru
One can never have too much glue

Pinterest boards all fill my head with ideas
Glitter and thread are all signs I was here - woooh

Crafter here - here I go again
Supplies - how can I resist you?
Take all year - going slow again
Cause I've too much to commit to

My home is taken over
Spouse is losing composure
But I've got to be creative

No idea when I'll get one done
Why, why do I start another?
Yes, it's clear, I'm the only one
Who'll start new projects forever

Crafter here - here I go again
Tie dye - how can I resist you?
More ideas - gotta sew again
Buy, buy! Or one day I'll miss you

When I am feeling frazzled
Random things get bedazzled
Why, my crafting mess just seems to grow
Now it's clear, now I really know
No, I'll never let this clutter go...

Piano Man / Trailers & Caravans

Original by Billy Joel

It's nine o'clock on a Saturday
I've been at the boat ramp since 3
I just wanted to sail but it's to no avail
And now there's a crowd watching me

They say, "straighten out, change your trajectory"
I'm not really sure how it goes
There's a queue down the street,
I give up - can't compete
Defeated, unsailed, I drive home

La, la-la, di-di-da La-la di-di-da da-dum

Keep me from trailers and caravans
I can't reverse them right
'Cause the angles and turns get the best of me
I'm backwards and forwards all night

I'm here in my car, and not feeling fine
More like a guilty escapee
My trailer's down the road, filled up with a big load
But it got the better of me

I got stuck when I backed and something gave a crack
Bloody fire hydrant got in the way
I might go back someday, but for now, stay away
I've done enough damage today

La, la-la, di-di-da La-la di-di-da da-dum

**Keep me from trailers and caravans
I can't reverse them right
'Cause the angles and turns get the best of me
And now I'm all stuck and jackknifed**

I was so pumped up for my big holiday
I've been needing a break for a while
Got a cute caravan and a map and a plan
To chill at the seaside in style

Found a picturesque glade with a view and some shade
I've blocked out how the next bit went
But suffice it to say, my best plans were mislaid
And now I'm sleeping in a tent

La, la-la, di-di-da La-la di-di-da da-dum

**Keep me from trailers and caravans
I can't reverse them right
'Cause the angles and turns get the best of me
I'd better let someone else drive**

Respect / Retract

Original by Aretha Franklin

What you want
(Meow) Kitty, I got it
(Meow) What you need
(Meow) You know I got it
(Meow) All I'm askin'
(Meow) Is for you to retract your claws at home (just a little bit)
Hey Kitty (just a little bit) oh, poor chair arm
(I really like it) That hurts! (I don't wanna quit)

I won't ever do you wrong while you're home
Ain't had my couches long (Meow) 'but still you're gonna (Meow)
All I'm askin' (Meow)
Is for you to retract - leave them alone (just a little bit)
Kitty (I really like it) don't want them torn (but they're better split)
No! (I will not submit)

See, furniture costs - a whole lot of money
And all I'm asking in return, Honey
Is to contain - your scratches
Leave chairs alone (just a, just a, just a, just a)
No, Kitty (just a, just a, just a, just a)
Don't want them torn (just a little bit)
No! (just a little bit)

Ooo, your kisses (Meow)
Sweeter than honey (Meow)
And guess what? (Meow)
So is my money (Meow)
All I want you to do (Meow) for me
Is to be nice to the things in my home (re, re, re, re)
No, Kitty (re, re, re, re)
Keep them claw-free (Retract? I can't handle it)
Respect my home, now (just a little bit)

R-E-T-R-A-C-T
Those sharp claws from my settee
R-E-T-R-A-C-T
A catastrophe!

Oh (I stick 'em in and sharpen 'em, I
Stick 'em in and sharpen 'em, I)
Have some respect (Don't care if you can't handle 'em
I stick 'em in and sharpen 'em)
Whoa, cat (just a little bit)

Please just retract (just a little bit)
I get tired (just a little bit)
You keep on tearin' (just a little bit)
My stuff's gettin' shredded (just a little bit)
And I ain't lyin' (just a little bit)

Retract (just a little bit)
Respect my home (just a little bit)
Mangled and broken (just a little bit)
This just isn't on! (just a little bit)
You love to scratch (just a little bit)
My home is now wrecked! (just a little bit)
Please retract!

Rolling In The Deep / Folding Fitted Sheets

Original by Adele

I'm so tired - my home's falling apart
Cleaning it feverishly, I still cannot make my mark
Want to see all my glassware crystal clear
No-one-said it's a workout to stop the wear and tear

See how I work to keep things shiny, new
I overestimated things that I could do
I'm just tired - my home's in entropy
Did not think household chores was a skill needing a degree

The stars just show off
Their homes and gardens
They keep me thinking
I don't have a clue at all
The stars all just love to
Keep things spotless
I can't help feeling

I can't do it at all
Folding fitted sheets
I try to but in spite
Of my plans
I can't make them
Nice and neat

Duvet inner's all clumped up, stuck and rolled
All night, my torso burns while my feet stick out all cold
Think of me cleaning drain holes from long hair
I gag and cannot look, a terrible nightmare

The stars have powers
They're far beyond us
Maybe they're hiring
Cleaning teams to do it all
I'm scarred, it's fruitless
My home's a big mess
I can't help feeling

I can't do it at all
Mowing down these weeds
I try to but in spite
Of my plans
I can't make it
All retreat

I can't do it at all
Keep my oven clean
I try to but in spite
Of my plans
When I bake, it
Spells defeat

Oh, my goal is white laundry, no more pink
Desks with no water rings, no oil clogging up my sink
Invent carpet that hides away all stains
Trash that takes itself out - cause I'll forget again!

I can't do this at all!
I can't do this at all!
At all, at all, at all!

I can't do it at all
Dusting makes me sneeze
I try to but in spite
Of my plans
Surfaces feel
Like a beach

I can't do it all
Housework's got me beat!
I try to but in spite
Of my plans
I'm afraid it, afraid it, afraid it
Is just too hard for me!

She's Got The Look / She Cannot Cook

Original by Roxette

Cupboards full of cans
Microwaves her dinner
Mostly eats bread and jam
Knows the take-out's number
Makes her boiled eggs pop
She cannot cook

Toast is too browned
She struggles boiling water
There's no salt to be found
Why's nobody taught her?
She's lost inside a food shop
She cannot cook

She cannot cook (She cannot cook)
She cannot cook (She cannot cook)
How in the world can you make pasta taste like glue?
And you need water with your meat when you make stew
And I go nah nah nah nah nah - she cannot cook

Overcooks her rice
Makes a kind of concrete
When she offers you pie
Run away - DO NOT EAT!
T'least she can pour cereal
She cannot cook

Really should be banned
From any kind of kitchen
When she offers a hand
Just point her to the dishes
Must protect your tastebuds
She cannot cook

She cannot cook (She cannot cook)
She cannot cook (She cannot cook)
What in the world has made this soup so tough to chew?
Do anything to stay away from her fondue
And I go nah nah nah nah nah -

Na na na na na na….
She cannot cook

She goes (na na na na na na)
She cannot cook

She cannot cook (She cannot cook)
She cannot cook (She cannot cook)
She cannot cook (She cannot cook)
She cannot cook (oh no-oo-oh-oo-oh)

Na na na na na na
She cannot cook

Na na na na na na
She cannot cook
She cannot cook!

Sound Of Silence / Sound Of Science

Original by Simon & Garfunkel

Hello darkness, my old friend
Each evening, here you come again
They say it's due to the earth rotating
That can't be true cause I don't feel a thing
There'd be collisions - oh, why don't they use their brains?
It's just insane
There's nothing sound in science

They say there's holes in the ozone
Why can't I see them from my home?
- Don't get me started on gravity
It's all such nonsense, just look up and see
Or else birds would fall, planes would crash from the sky mid-flight
Does that seem right?
You're just too bound by science

And with my own two eyes I saw
The first red leaves of autumn fall
And now you tell me half the world's in spring?
Dude, look around you, you must be joking!
I knew all along that scientists are weird
Yet they're revered
Don't like the sound of science

"Fools" said I, "Everyone knows
Sun's from the earth's core cause it rose"
Look around - let what you see teach you
Ditch the books, don't let them reach you
Mark my words, or you'll spout their crap as well
You'll be swallowed in that hell of science

The best thing now to do is pray
For logic to go away
Is that a critical thought forming?
Whatcha doing?! Heed my warning!
It is time to stop thinking at all
Keep your world small
And do not stick around for science

Stairway To Heaven / What A Cat Would Sing

Original by Led Zeppelin

There's a way to be sure that I walk out the door
What is this in my bowl I've been given?
I will turn up my nose, have you smelled it? It's gross.
Hurry up, give me food that I care for

Ooh, ooh - I'm not trying it - gotta be kidding!

Look for signs when I purr while you're stroking my fur
Just let go when you see my tail twitching
Yes, I'll sit in the door for a minute or more
Why be mad when I take my time thinking?

Ooh, it makes me wonder
Ooh, why you blunder

There's a feeling I get when I've been out, got wet
So I rub up against you for drying
No, don't go get a towel, do you want me to howl?
Just let me on your lap and get stroking

Ooh, it makes me wonder
Ooh, why you blunder

You might say, "I love you," but just look what you do
Do you even consider my feelings?
I show you all along what you need to get done
But it's like you just don't understand me

Oh-oh-oh-oh-whoa

If there is something in my litter box, clean it up now
Make it squeaky clean, fit for your queen
You have two seconds to change my water, human, come on
Then I'll walk away, you took too long

And it makes me wonder
Ohh, whoa

I might want something, and you're meant to know, so do not be slow
You're my butler, so meet my needs
And lady, don't expect tomorrow, I'll want the same, no
That's just the joy of loving me

So you want a happy kitty?
Then anticipate all my needs
Know when to stroke or leave me be
It doesn't take a PHD
To see your purpose - care for me

Just put me first, is it that hard?
You'll get a purr from me at last
If you do all I want you to
I'll spend all my nine lives with you

But what's this in my bowl I've been given?

Take My Breath Away / Take My Bread Away
Original by Berlin

Wafting from the oven, infiltrates my hungry brain
Freshly made cakes, muffins, sources of my secret shame
I'm now salivating - longing to be satisfied
Turning in slow motion, shake my head and sadly say

Take my bread away
Take my bread away

I'm not advocating banning all the foods I love
But it's aggravating how I'm not the size I was
When I smell toast burning, secretly I smile inside
It quells my devotion, makes it easier to say - "Enough"

Take my bread away

Once an hourglass before you, more like a ball today
Carbohydrates, I'll ignore you, you make my stomach pay
So, please stay out my way - don't lead me astray

Take my bread away
Take my bread away

If there were a lotion that could make all smells the same
Then I'd get the notion - to like cabbage, freshly baked
But I keep returning - bakeries just make me cry
Master my emotions - takes all that I have - to say

Take my bread away
Enough - Take my bread away
Enough - Take my bread away -Enough
Enough - Take my bread away

Take On Me / Cat Version

Original by A-ha

I'm darting away
All that noise, how'm I to stay
Thanks for ruining my day
There is never a good time to vacuum Hide it away
To be worthy of my love, okay?

Take on me
(Tame kitty)
Take me on
(Not pretty)
I'll be gone
Where will that leave you?

This needless delay
We won't be friends
If you make me - meow at my plate
Know me, person - that brand's not okay
That's so last week
I don't want that food today, not sorry!

Take on me
(Tame kitty)
Take me on
(Not pretty)
I'll be gone
Then what will you do?

Oh, you're going out today yeah?
Hang on, YIKES! You've got my crate - NO!
Put it away!
Do you want me to hate you forever?
I'm hissing away
What's a vet? Don't like the sound of 'spayed'

Take on me
(Tame kitty)
Take me on
(Not pretty)
I'll be gone
Be nice to me!

Take on me
(Tame kitty)
Take me on
(Not pretty)
You're my one!
The one for me!

The Logical Song / Dog Version

Original by Supertramp

When you were young, you thought that life was so wonderful,
A miracle, oh, it was beautiful, magical
But by the time you got me, your joy seemed smothered in atrophy
Catastrophe, lackadaisically, not like me

Oh, person, just look my way, I'll teach you how to be jovial,
Excitable, oh, enjoyable, casual
Learn to stop being concerned about how to be presentable
Respectable, oh, ostensible, it's terrible

Take some time to curl up for a sleep
Don't stress or think too deep
Forget your complex plans

Just relax, with belly in the air
And snore without a care
While under patting hands

I said, now, go out and play, it's your calling to chase that ball
Go for a walk, splash in puddles, get cuddles
Oh, no two days are the same when you see life as a smorgasbord
Get all aboard, love and be adored, can't get bored

My tail will shake it, yeah

Every night, I snuggle you to sleep
I feel your warmth with me
That's all I need each day
Won't you please
Enjoy the here and now
Watch me, I'll show you how
Delight in food, love, play
Every day
Life is great
Whatcha waiting for? - Be like me

Because all life can be magical
Yeah
W w w w w w w wonderful
Makes your tail wiggle

Time After Time / Time Flies Online

Original by Cyndi Lauper

Lying in my bed, I'm here on TikTok and YouTube too
Caught up in scrolling
It's movement, so I am glued
Flashback, old times, when I went outside
Device free memories
Time flies on

Sometimes I watch TV
While browsing the internet
You're calling to me, I can't hear
What you've said
Locked away, screen glow
Has numbed my mind
Reality unwinds

I am lost, I just look at a moving screen
Time flies online
Tend to fall, bump and crash cause I'm not looking
Time flies online

You can do what you want, it won't bother me
Time flies online
Cause I'm stuck in another reality
Time flies online

After my battery fades, I'm plunged into life today
Stare into nothing
You're wondering if I'm okay
Furtive glances at life outside
What is it really like?

I am lost, I just look at a moving screen
Time flies online
Just a blink and a thumb scroll show I'm living
Time flies online

If you call while I'm browsing, won't hear a thing
Time flies online
If my phone were to die, well, I would be mourning
Time flies online

Locked away, screen glow
Has numbed my mind
Reality unwinds

I am locked, catatonic behind my screen
Time flies online
Wait for internet outage to talk to me
Time flies online

Like a zombie, I'm hooked to technology
Time flies online
Battery fails, I will charge you - don't keep me waiting!
Time flies online

Time flies online
I can't untwine
There's no use tryin'
You see that I'm
On a flatline
Can't see the signs
I'm just denyin'
That time online
Is my decline
Time flies online

Time Of My Life / Prime Of My Life

Original by Bill Medley & Jennifer Warnes

Have I passed the prime of my life?
No, I've never felt like this before
I'm aware I'm no youth
But I know what I can do

They say I've passed the prime of my life
But have I got news for you….

I've been living for so long
Now I'm finally someone I like to be
See, now I don't care at all
'bout what I wear to the mall - I'm comfy!

Now I do just what I like
You don't get it? Take a hike - it don't bother me
I have got the upper hand
'Cause I've been there, understand, got history

Just remember
You're a young thing
That will fade soon enough
So I'll tell you something
Old meat is tough because

I'm at the prime of my life
No, I've never felt this way before
I'm aware I'm no youth
But just watch what I can do

Old lady!

As my body grows older
I laugh more than you'll ever know
Like a wine time has grown
Or well aged cheese, I now feel whole, oh
And these wrinkles, spots and lines
Are all signs that life's been alright! (Sing with me!)

Just remember
Age is one thing
That-really doesn't mean much
So I'll tell you something
Do what you love because

I'm at the prime of my life
No, I've never been this age before
Cause who cares what you do?
It's your time for being you!

Cause I'm at the prime of my life
No, I've never felt like this before
I'm aware I'm no youth
But worn in's better than new

Now I'm at the prime of my life
No, I've never been this age before
Get out there - just be you
Give them one to look up to

I'm at the prime of my life
No, I've never felt this way before
Yes, I'm here - not just youth
I can make my mark here too

I'm at the prime of my life
No, I've never been this age before
Cause who cares what you do?
It's your time for being you!

Time Warp / Time Worn

Original by Nell Campbell, Patricia Quinn, and Richard O'Brien

It's astounding
Time is fleeting
Wrinkles take their toll
Must read things closely
Can't stay awake much longer
I'm trying to keep control
Don't remember feeling so time worn
Remembering those moments when
Night time wouldn't hit me
Now, instead, my bed's calling

I'm feeling time worn again
I'm feeling time worn again

I've got no energy left
And I can't sleep through the night
Getting jams in my hips
And gotta clench real tight
Put out my back, it just
Can really drive me insane

I'm feeling time worn again
I'm feeling time worn again

Youth was dreamy
Decrepitude, free me
I hate to see me
Feeling haggard and small
This feels like a detention
I need more gas in my engine
Get me rebooted
To do all

Had a bit of a mind flip
Don't know where I left it
My body won't ever be the same
Get these aches and sensations
I'm spaced on medication

I'm feeling time worn again
I'm feeling time worn again

Once, I was nimble on my feet, and oh the things that I could think
And I could stay up all night and wouldn't sleep a wink
Time's shaken me up, it's been a big surprise
I've got hours on the clock, but I'm not feelin' wise
It's wearing me - I don't like this change
Time is rushing - take me back to old days!

I'm feeling time worn again
I'm feeling time worn again

I've got no energy left
And I can't sleep through the night
Wear my pants past my hips
And got the worst eyesight
But it's my sagging bust
That really drives me insane

I'm feeling time worn again
I'm feeling time worn again

Total Eclipse Of The Heart / Song For Older People

Original by Bonnie Tyler

Slowing down
Every now and then I feel a little bit useless
Thinking back when I was wild
Slowing down
Every now and then I feel a little bit helpless
When I find I've got no strength in my arms
Slowing down
Every now and then I get a little bit angry
When it seems the world is passing me by
Slowing down
Every now and then I get a little bit gasified
If I eat too much bread or French fries

Slowing down - time flies
Every now and then I fall apart
Slowing down - time flies
Feels as if I am falling apart

And I want to sleep tonight
And I want stable blood pressure
And to go back to good eyesight
Not have skin that feels like leather
And not wake up as soon as it's light
And feel healthy and strong

It's feeling like my energy has hit a flatline
I'd love to find the vigour that I had back in time (youth was sublime)
I don't know what to do - I need more than a face mask
I'm easily exhausted by the simplest of tasks

Please let me sleep through the night
They say the future's looking bright
But I feel like a troglodyte

Once upon a time I was sharp, fierce and tough
But now I'm simply falling apart
(Low) There's nothing I can do
I pee just a bit when I laugh

Once upon a time I felt youthful and bright
But now I'm stumbling 'round in the dark
I'm ashamed to say
I'm scared to commit to a fart
I might do a bit more than fart

This is my demise
Ageing is not nice - gets me down

Vincent / Vintage

Original by Don McLean

Staying up all night
Can't keep nature's calls at bay
Longing for the break of day
Despise my bladder, like a leaking bowl

Then there's all the pills
A smorgasbord for all my ills
I'm scared to sneeze in case of spills
This ageing thing is getting out of hand

Now I understand
What my body's saying to me
I'm succumbing now to gravity
I've got furniture disease
My chest is slipping, I do not know how
It's gone to my drawers now

Staying up all night
Flaming more than hellfire's blaze
Clammy sheets, my mind's a haze
I kick them off, then freeze - what else to do?
I wish that I could sue
Good Lord above, it's poor design
To have us creak and age with time
I think it's time to update factory plans

Now I understand
What my body's saying to me
That with age comes more insanity
Won't my body let me be?
It will not listen, this is not a drill
I'm now over the hill

Vogue / Vague

Original by Madonna

I don't know
Vague
Vague

Look around, everyone knows what they're doing
It's everywhere that I go
I try everything I can to fit in
Not let on what I don't know

When all else fails and they look to me
Then I cannot give myself away
I've mastered hiding I don't know a thing
I'll be a talk bore
And they'll be no more the wiser

I am vague
They have no idea that I'm clueless - Hey, hey, hey
Really vague
Say big words, pretend that I know - Confidence will do it

All I need is to learn from television
And keep some big words in store
Make wise eyes, frown to add authentication
Then let the baloney pour

It makes no difference if the newspeak is right
Just makes me sound real mature
Get those phrases pumping, like I've got this insight
I look super smart
Yes, it's a fine art - I own it

I am vague
I just rattle off things oft repeated - Hey, hey, hey
Really vague
Act all cocky, put on a show - Confidence will do it

Want to hear the things I know?
Can't reveal that I'm shallow
Topic too hard for my plate?
I just discombobulate

Climate change - my position?
State redundant axioms
Pressing issues? War and crime?
Let's divest our paradigm

Crypto, NFTs, blockchains?
Think sesquipedalian
Smile, evade, circumlocute
They'll never catch onto you

Like the emperor with no clothes
They'll be hoodwinked - think I know
Don't just stand there, let's get to it
None will guess that I am clueless

Vague, vague
Vague, vague
Vague, vague
Vague, vague

Ooh, I don't know
Act all cocky - bluff my way through it
Ooh, I've got to just
Use the biggest words that I know
Ooh, I'm really just
Vague (vague, vague, vague…)

Wake Me Up Before You Go-Go / Song For Introverts

Original by Wham!

Another chatterbox
The small talk never stops
I've really had enough
I hate this social stuff

The music boom-booms, hearing is hard (ooh-ooh)
And then this old, weird guy
Sidles up and starts
Chatterboxing - it's inane (yeah yeah)
Don't care what he's saying
Energy's being drained

This party's bugging me
Does not excite
Not my best way to
Spend a happy night

I could be sleeping in my bed
What was I thinking
I should've stayed at home instead

Had enough! I want to go, go
They're always banging on - I'm stuck in slow-mo
Beam me up! - I want to go, go
I hate this whole visit - could curl up and die
It's too much! - I want to go, go
What's wrong with spending an evening solo
Had enough! I want to go, go - ah
Back to sweat pants tonight
Don't wanna chit-chat - BYE! Yeah, yeah

Don't want to socialise - get outta my way (ooh-ooh)
What makes it fun at night - I've worked with them all day?
And when it gets dark, I can't be blamed (yeah-yeah)
My sleep is worth much more than this social pain

It drives me crazy
It's not cool
I'm back to games of fitting in at school

I'll be lazy
That's alright
You go dancing
I'm happier home tonight

Had enough! I want to go, go
They're always banging on - I'm stuck in slow-mo
Beam me up! - I want to go, go
Hate this whole visit - wanna curl up and die
It's too much! - I want to go, go
What's wrong with spending an evening solo
Had enough! I want to go, go
Back to sweat pants tonight
Don't wanna chit-chat - BYE! Yeah, yeah, yeah, don't make me

Another chatterbox
I hate this social stuff

Got my fur baby
I'm alright
You go partying, I'm fine tonight
It's cold out there
But it's warm in bed
You can dance and
I'll stay home instead

Chatterbox

Had enough! I want to go, go
They're always banging on - I'm stuck in slow-mo
Beam me up! - I want to go, go
I hate this all - just wanna curl up and die
It's too much! - I want to go, go
What's wrong with spending an evening solo
Had enough! I want to go, go, ah
Back to sweat pants tonight

Don't leave me here - they're banging on
- I am stuck in slow-mo, mo, mo
Back to sweat pants
Alone in my room - oh
It's what I want to do
Yeah, yeah, yeah
ooh-aah
Yeah

Walking On Sunshine / Song About Ageing

Original by Katrina & The Waves

I used to think ageing was ugly, now, baby, I'm sure
But I won't get dragged down by things I can't do any more
I'm rusty and creaky from hard knocks - why should that hold me down?
Why not celebrate? Each day's great when I'm not in the ground

Not aged like a fine wine - no
I'm covered in laugh lines - whoa
My body's in decline - oh
But I'm gonna feel good!
Hey, all right now
I choose to feel good!
Hey, yeah

I used to think ageing might bug me, now I know that it's true
It's not fun - to keep finding - more things - that are harder to do
Now, it seems like I reach for my wheat bag for new aches every day, oh, oh, oh
I feel shaky and put out my back, but I'm still here to play! - oh yeah now

I'm owning my waistline - whoa
And receding hairline - no
But still I'm on Cloud Nine
Cause I'm gonna feel good!
Hey, all right now
I choose to feel good!

Yeah, oh, yeah, now
I'm feeling so good
Been 'round a long time
Won't sit on the sidelines

I'm still alive, it's kinda rough, now I'm tired of - being made to feel
That I can't thrive, oh, stop that guff, I've become tough - I'm got zeal
Age don't define me, baby, no!
Oh, yeah - 'm on Cloud Nine, baby

Not aged like a fine wine - no
I'm covered in laugh lines - whoa
My body's in decline - oh
But I'm gonna feel good!
Hey, all right now
I choose to feel good!

I'll say it, I'll say it, I'll say it again now
I choose to feel good!
I'm gonna, gonna, gonna, gonna, gonna,,
I'm gonna feel good!
Now tell me, tell me, what was I saying now?
Ooh - that don't feel good

Okay - OW!
I'm not feeling good!
Oh, cramp, cramp, cramp, cramp - aah - don't touch me!
Think I'm going to lie down
Oh, yeah, oh, yeah, oh, yeah
Could you turn that noise down?
Oh, yeah, yeah, yeah, oh, yeah, oh, yeah
And don't it feel good
I'll say it, I'll say it, I'll say it again now
I'm feeling so good

Yesterday / Use-By Date

Original by The Beatles

Yesterday, oh, I should have checked the use-by date
Now I've got more food to throw away
Should have been eaten yesterday

Broccoli - at least I think that's what this used to be
This potato's growing like a tree
Their use-by dates came suddenly

Spoiled avocado
Yes, I know, it's such a waste
Jam has fizz, tastes strong
Now I long for yesterday

Yesterday, this was a tomato, not puree
Now I bite bread, but it won't give way
Crept up on me, the use-by date

Mould's starting to grow
So no-go, throw it away
My milk smells quite wrong
Now I long for yesterday

Yesterday, my fridge wasn't filled with such decay
Sour cream now looks like crème brûlée
Should have been eaten yesterday

Mmmmmmmmmm

YMCA / Why Menstruate?

Original by The Village People

Young man, if we look kinda down
I said, young man, pimples, cramps and a frown
I said, young man, best to not stick around
We might make you quite unhappy

Young man, you have not got a clue
I said, young man, what our bodies all do
You just get back, and I'm sure you will find
We'll come right in a few days' time

And every month we cry - Why menstruate?
Feel like we're gonna die - Why menstruate?
Yes, the science is clear, but this seems so severe
Just be grateful that you are boys!

Each month for most our lives - Why menstruate?
Your daughters, mums and wives - Why menstruate?
When you get a nose bleed, we have no sympathy -
This is like a Biblical plague!

Young man, are you listening to me?
I said, young man, when I'm sore and grumpy
You don't like it, but I hate it far more
Get me chocolate before I roar!

Shark Week every month of my life
Down there, bleeding, more than 400 times
So don't go there, saying I'll be okay
Rub my back, then just go away

Poor women cramp and cry - Why menstruate?
Another month goes by - Why menstruate?
Yet another egg's flushed - out to make some more space
For a new one - what a big waste!

So just get out my way - Why menstruate?
Each month for a few days - Why menstruate?
Like old battery hens, we feel tired and abused
But not one of these eggs are used!

Young man, put yourself in our shoes
No, don't - you'll faint, you just haven't a clue
You're bad enough when you've got the man flu
This would be far too much for you

Some say we should be glad that we
Get to form life from eggs into babies
But most women will have 1, 2 or 3
Yet each month we go through this pain

There's bad design at play - Why menstruate?
Each month, there is decay - Why menstruate?
While we deal with the mess, it's just like a crime scene
You had better treat us like queens!

Why menstruate?
Just feed us chocolate now - Why menstruate?
Young man, young man, you have got no idea
Young man, young man, when our cycle is here

Why menstruate?
This is a horror movie - Why menstruate?
Young man, women need you to keep at bay
Young man, keep clear each month for a few days

You Don't Own Me / Cat Version

Original by Lesley Gore

You don't own me
I'm not just one of your little toys
You don't own me
Don't think I won't do what brings ME joy

And don't tell me what to do
Don't try to make me stay
And please, when I come head-butt you
Meet my needs right away 'cause

You don't own me
Don't try to change me in any way
You don't own me
Don't hold me down 'cause I'll never stay

A dog lives to make your day
A dog asks you what to do
But me? Let me lick myself
I'll call when I need you

I'll come when I decide to come
I'm free and I love to be free
I live my life the way I want
To scratch, explore wherever I please

You don't own me
So just be grateful I stick around
You don't own me
But you're the best butler I have found

So don't tell me what to do
And don't try to make me stay
And please, when I low growl at you
Hands off - get out my way

It's fun how you think that I'll come
P(urrr)lease - I just love to be free
Be grateful you're the one
I chose you to meet my needs

You're The One That I Want / Money Song

Original by John Travolta & Olivia Newton-John

I got bills, they're multiplying
And I'm losing control
Phone and power've got me crying
It's intensifying

The debt is way up
Now I need a plan
Can't afford anything new
Goodbye to make up
All my nice treats are banned
Shopping malls give me the blues
Nothin' left, all my spending days are through

You're the one that I want (you are the one I want) Ooh, ooh, ooh, money
You're the one that I want (you are the one I want) Ooh, ooh, ooh, money
You're the one that I want (you are the one I want) Ooh, ooh, ooh
A ton I need, Oh, yes, indeed

Need to take a collection
Please donate - help me pay
'Cause I'd like a cash injection
Need Pay Day (Wow!)

I better pay up
'Cause I need my van
Full of fuel so I can ride
I've gotta weigh up
Every single plan
Will the cost be justified?
Are you sure
That you need your hair blow dried?

You're the one that I want (you are the one I want) Ooh, ooh, ooh, money
You're the one that I want (you are the one I want) Ooh, ooh, ooh, money
You're the one that I want (you are the one I want) Ooh, ooh, ooh
A ton I need, Oh, yes, indeed

You're the one that I want (you are the one I want) Ooh, ooh, ooh, money
You're the one that I want (you are the one I want) Ooh, ooh, ooh, money
You're the one that I want (you are the one I want) Ooh, ooh, ooh
A ton I need, Oh, yes, indeed

Thank you for singing along with my silly lyrics!
Make sure to subscribe to my YouTube channel,
because I never know when a new song will come!

www.youtube.com/@ShirleySerban

Did you want your own, personalised parodied song, or an original, for a special occasion, someone you love, or to just treat yourself? I would love to help you. Get in touch through my website or by email:

www.shirleycan.com
shirley@shirleycan.com

Thanks!

Printed in Great Britain
by Amazon